This
**F**rog **book**
**belongs to:**

.....................................

This paperback edition first published in 2014 by Andersen Press Ltd.

20 Vauxhall Bridge Road, London SW1V 2SA.

First published in Great Britain in 2002 by Andersen Press Ltd.

Published in Australia by Random House Australia Pty.,

20 Alfred Street, Milsons Point, Sydney, NSW 2061.

Copyright © Foundation Max Velthuijs, 2002.

Colour separated in Switzerland by Photolitho AG, Zürich.

Printed and bound in China by Foshan Zhaorong Printing Co., Ltd.

10    9    8    7    6    5    4    3    2    1

British Library Cataloguing in Publication Data available.

ISBN 978 1 78344 151 8

# Frog and the Treasure

## Max Velthuijs

Andersen Press

"Let's hurry up and finish our breakfast, Little Bear,"
said Frog. "Today we are going to dig for treasure!"
"Dig for treasure?" said Little Bear. "What does that
mean?"
"Come with me and you'll find out," said Frog.

"We are going to dig a deep hole," he explained.
"We are going to dig and dig, until we find treasure."
"But what if there isn't any treasure?" said Little Bear.
"There is always treasure," said Frog. "I promise."

All at once, Frog stopped and pointed at the ground.
"This is where we'll find treasure," he said. "Right here!"
"How do you know?" said Little Bear.
"I just *know*," said Frog.

Frog started to dig. Little Bear watched, full of admiration.
It looked very hard work.
Soon enough, Frog was tired. "Now it's your turn, Little
Bear," he said.
Little Bear wasn't sure, but he took the spade . . .

. . . and bravely he began to dig. But the spade was far too big and much too heavy for him.
"This is useless," said Frog after a while. "We'll never find treasure at this rate. Give it back to me."

So Little Bear watched while Frog dug, deeper and deeper – until he could hardly be seen.
"Frog!" called Little Bear. "Is there any treasure yet?"

"No, not yet . . ." came Frog's voice from far below.
"Careful, Little Bear, here comes a stone . . ."
But Little Bear couldn't hear. He leant over into
the hole, and . . .

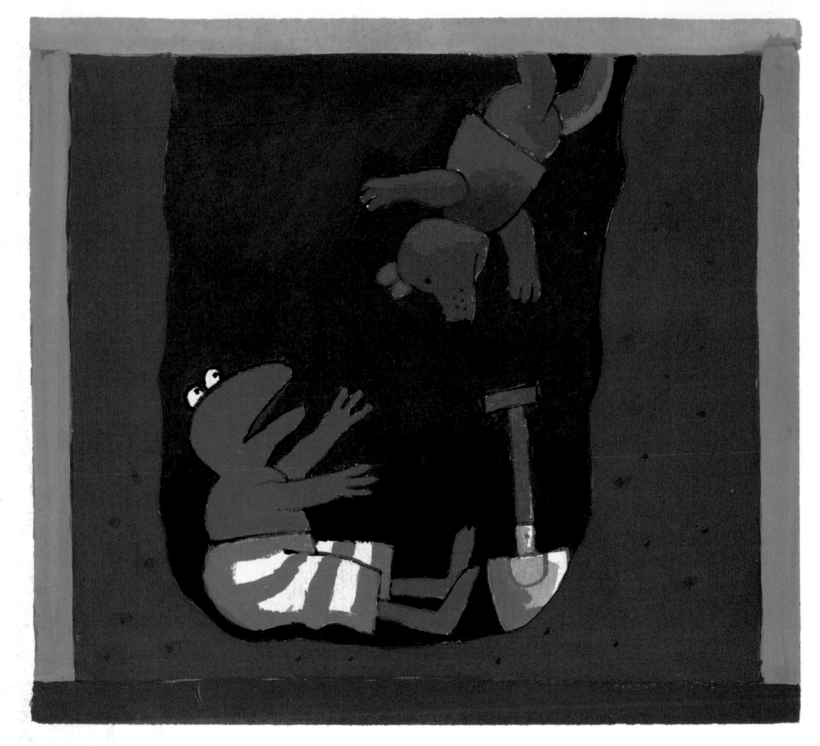

. . . in he fell!
There they sat in the deep, dark hole.
"I'm hungry," said Little Bear. "I want to go home."
"We can't," said Frog, quietly. "This hole is too deep.
We can't climb out. We're trapped."
Little Bear started to cry. "We'll be here forever!" he wept

"I'll never go fishing with Rat again and Hare will miss
me so!"
Frog was scared, too. He didn't know how to
comfort Little Bear. "Be brave, Little Bear," he said.
"Let's shout for help. Someone is sure to hear." So they
called and called – but nobody came.

Then Frog had another idea. "Let's sing," he said. "Let's sing a sitting-in-the-hole song to cheer ourselves up." The moon rose, the night came.

Frog and Little Bear sang and sang, until they were
so tired that they slept, even though they were far
away from their own warm, little bed . . .

Early next morning, Duck was out for a walk
when she came across a mountain of sand.
"How very curious!" she exclaimed. "This wasn't
here yesterday!"
Then she saw the hole and went to find Pig.

Pig leant over and called down into the hole, "Hello?
Is anybody there?"
"Yes, we are!" shouted Frog and Little Bear together.
"It's us. Frog and Little Bear! We can't get out!"
"I think we should go and fetch Rat," said Pig.

Duck hurried off, shouting at the top of her voice.
"Rat! Rat, come quickly! Frog and Little Bear are
trapped in a hole and they can't get out!"

Rat knew exactly what to do. He fetched a ladder from the barn and he and Duck hurried to the scene of the disaster.

Rat lowered the ladder into the hole, which was so deep that soon the ladder disappeared. "Climb up, Little Bear!" called the animals. "And Frog, you must follow! Don't be scared. We'll help you out!"

Carefully, Little Bear started to climb.
When he was close enough to the top of the hole,
his friends pulled him to safety.
Then it was Frog's turn . . .

Everyone cheered when Frog's head appeared above the ground. "Hooray!" they shouted, as Rat helped him out of the hole.

"But what were you doing down there?" asked Hare, anxiously. "Such a deep hole is extremely dangerous. We must fill it in at once."

"It was me," said Frog quietly. "I promised Little Bear we would find treasure but there was none. Now there's just a big, useless hole and it's all my fault." Frog was so disappointed.

"Ah, but you did find treasure," said Rat solemnly, kneeling down and picking up the stone lying nearby. "This stone is more than a hundred million years old!"

He polished the stone on his sleeve until it gleamed.
Then he handed it to Frog.
Frog could hardly believe his eyes. He beamed with
pleasure.

"Thank you, Rat," he said, proudly. "But I think this is Little Bear's treasure. I shall give it to him – because he was so brave, and because I promised!"

**Max Velthuijs's** twelve beautiful stories about **Frog** and his friends first started to appear twenty five years ago and are now available as paperbacks, e-books and apps.

**Max Velthuijs** (Dutch for Field House) lived in the Netherlands, and received the prestigious Hans Christian Andersen Medal for Illustration. His charming stories capture childhood experiences while offering life lessons to children as young as three, and have been translated into more than forty languages.

'Frog is an inspired creation — a masterpiece of graphic simplicity.'
**GUARDIAN**

'Miniature morality plays for our age.' **IBBY**